SEMINOLE DIARY
Remembrances of a Slave

DOLORES JOHNSON

Macmillan Publishing Company   New York
Maxwell Macmillan Canada   Toronto
Maxwell Macmillan International   New York   Oxford   Singapore   Sydney

In 1990, I began research on a story about slavery for an exhibit in a children's museum (which later became the book *Now Let Me Fly: The Story of a Slave Family*, published by Macmillan). It was then that I first became aware of the many rarely told stories of people who risked their lives and homes aiding African-American slaves in their escapes to freedom. I became determined to bring some of the stories to children and decided to tell these tales as fiction.

I would like to take this opportunity to acknowledge all those who helped me tell this particular story. Initially, I would like to thank Billy J. Cypress, executive director of the Seminole Museum in Hollywood, Florida, as well as members of the staff at the Historical Museum of Southern Florida. In California, I was tremendously assisted by the use of the libraries of the Southwest Museum and of Los Angeles County, and I would like to acknowledge all the librarians who helped me in my research. One librarian in particular, Robin Hunter of the Inglewood Public Library, offered me invaluable assistance and encouragement.

And again, I would like to offer thanks to my editor, Judith R. Whipple, and my art director, Jean Krulis, at Macmillan for helping me tell this story.

10 9 8 7 6 5 4 3 2 1

Library of Congress Cataloging-in-Publication Data   Johnson, Dolores. Seminole diary : remembrances of a slave / written and illustrated by Dolores Johnson. — 1st ed.   p.   cm.   ISBN 0-02-747848-3   1. Fugitive slaves—Juvenile literature.   2. Black Seminoles—Juvenile literature.   [1. Fugitive slaves.   2. Black Seminoles.   3. Seminole Indians.   4. Indians of North America.]   I. Title.   E450.J67 1994   975.9'00496073—dc20   94-4240   Summary: Libbie, a young African-American slave, escapes from a plantation in 1834 and is taken South to Florida to join the Seminole Indian tribe.

To my aunt, Elizabeth Mitchell

Gina found her mother in the attic, sitting by an open steamer trunk. Scattered on the floor at her feet lay a stack of paintings, a battered watch, a feather, straw baskets, and a doll wearing a brightly colored dress. Gina's mother didn't even look up when Gina entered the attic, she was so involved in reading from a worn, leather-bound book.

"What's that, Mom?" Gina asked as she picked up the doll from the floor.

Gina's mother looked at her daughter and smiled. "It's a present. It's a gift one of our ancestors handed down to us."

"Which ancestor?" asked Gina.

"A slave named Libbie. We're all so lucky she could read and write, because she left us with this treasure. I'm not talking about these beads, these baskets, or these paintings. Libbie left us with a wealth of precious memories that she wrote down in this book. She made a record of a time when there was a special relationship between two groups of people. It's a story that's rarely been told."

"Read it to me, Mom," said Gina. "I want to hear the story." Gina's mother opened the book and began to read.

Thursday, March 13, 1834

Master Evans whipped me kinda bad. I thought Papa was going to come apart, he was so mad. He told me, "Libbie, we ain't staying here no more. We joining the other slaves escaping this plantation. We going to freedom *tonight*."

Tuesday, April 1, 1834

Finally we arrive at a resting place. We been traveling both night and day. Ten of us crawl through thickets and trudge knee deep through marshes. Sometimes I beg Papa to let us go back. But he say, "My girls will never live another day as slaves. I'm a man, and I aim to live as one!"

But Clarissa ain't a man. She only seven. And I'm not that much older. And I get more dirty, tired, and hungry every step I take. It's hard to keep going when you don't even know where you're going. And why are we heading south when everybody knows you follow the North Star to freedom? Maybe it's 'cause Papa thinks Clarissa can't walk as far as Pennsylvania. It certainly can't be 'cause of me.

I got to go now. I hear dogs barking in the distance. Could be slave hunters. God save us all.

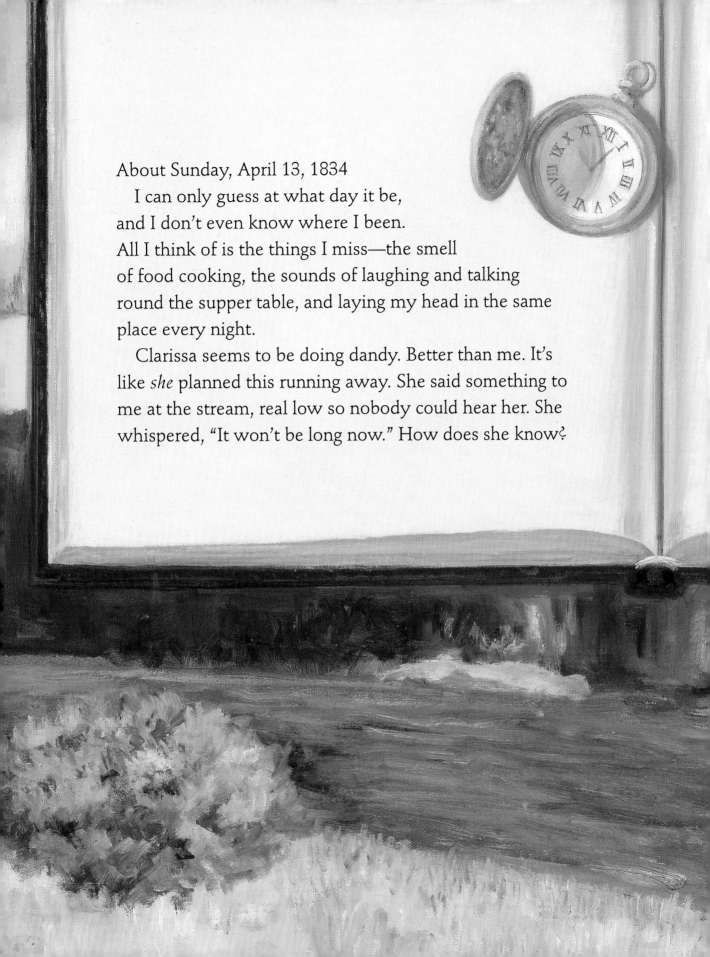

About Sunday, April 13, 1834

    I can only guess at what day it be,
and I don't even know where I been.
All I think of is the things I miss—the smell
of food cooking, the sounds of laughing and talking
round the supper table, and laying my head in the same
place every night.

    Clarissa seems to be doing dandy. Better than me. It's
like *she* planned this running away. She said something to
me at the stream, real low so nobody could hear her. She
whispered, "It won't be long now." How does she know?

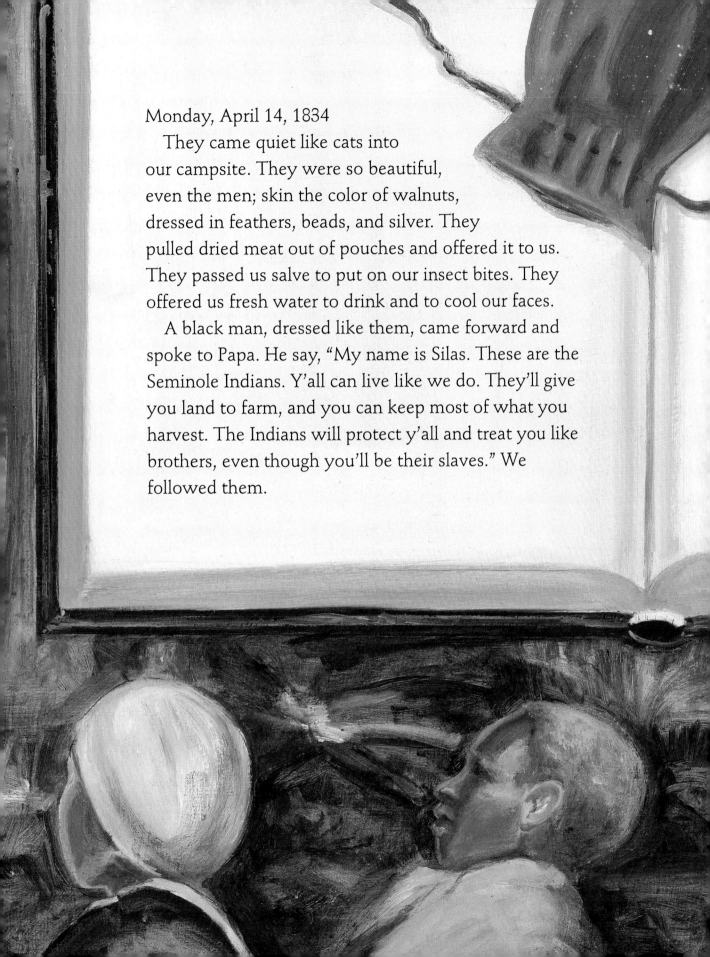

Monday, April 14, 1834
    They came quiet like cats into
our campsite. They were so beautiful,
even the men; skin the color of walnuts,
dressed in feathers, beads, and silver. They
pulled dried meat out of pouches and offered it to us.
They passed us salve to put on our insect bites. They
offered us fresh water to drink and to cool our faces.
    A black man, dressed like them, came forward and
spoke to Papa. He say, "My name is Silas. These are the
Seminole Indians. Y'all can live like we do. They'll give
you land to farm, and you can keep most of what you
harvest. The Indians will protect y'all and treat you like
brothers, even though you'll be their slaves." We
followed them.

Tuesday, April 15, 1834

Papa, as the leader of our group, met with the Seminole leader of the settlement. His name is Chief Running Tiger, and Papa seems to think he is a very fair man.

"Libbie," Papa told me, his eyes shining big and bright. "Them Seminoles respect us as human beings. But the chief say if we become *their* slaves, the slave catchers don't dare come take us from here.

"This is as safe as we'll ever be in the South, Libbie. I was so thankful, I tried to tell the chief every little thing I know. I warned him about every broken twig in the roads we just passed, every footprint, every horse's track. Maybe my warnings will help us all stay safe from them soldiers and settlers who are trying to steal this land."

Thursday, April 17, 1834

There is an Indian woman named Honey Flower who has taken a liking to Clarissa. Honey Flower's house has become Clarissa's house, and she treats my sister like part of her family. I can tell Papa don't like it. But Clarissa does. And that's all that counts for her.

Clarissa say, "Honey Flower lost her daughter when she was a baby. I told her how Mama died on the day I was born."

"How can y'all talk together?" I asked her. "You don't even speak the same language." Sometimes that girl don't make no sense at all.

"There are times folks can talk to each other without even using words," said Clarissa.

Monday, May 19, 1834

Clarissa ain't the same as she was. She's Indian now. She wears their clothes, their beads around her neck, and their moccasins. That girl's not a slave anymore.

But then again, I ain't neither. I sit with Clarissa at Honey Flower's knee and learn to speak and live and breathe the breaths of a Seminole woman.

The other slaves have made their homes here as well. We grow crops of corn, cotton, and sweet potatoes, and raise pigs, cows, and chickens. We eat coontie bread like the Indians and live in houses just like theirs. Our life is so different than life on the plantation. This joy can't last.

Saturday, June 14, 1834

Clarissa brought over an Indian boy to help with the harvest. Honey Flower told her, "Tending the fields is women's work. But men help with the harvesting." Thank goodness, 'cause Papa ain't around much anymore. He spends so much time off tending to Indian business.

The Indian boy, named Wild Jumper, is 'bout as old as me. He's a warrior—he told me so. And when we are resting and alone, he tells me so many things. But then sometimes he falls into a silence that's as dark and heavy as a grave. Isn't it funny? I only learned how to laugh since we been living with the Seminoles. But Seminole boys don't have time for that stuff. They have to be men.

Wednesday, June 25, 1834

Clarissa don't come around much anymore. And when she comes, she makes sure we call her Swift Sparrow. Papa can't bring hisself to call her that 'cause Clarissa was Mama's name.

When I finally caught her alone, I grabbed her hand and carried her away from Honey Flower. I pretended I needed her to search the plants and berries for pigments for my paintings. Then Clarissa sat and played with her doll while I drew pictures of my little Indian sister. But things ain't the same between us. It's like she had business to attend to, and not with me. So I let her go on.

Friday, June 27, 1834

Wild Jumper and I stood in the fields, checking to see if the corn was ready. I stripped a cob from its stalk and went to take a bite, when Wild Jumper pulled the corn away. "You can't eat that now," he say.

"Why not?" I ask. I was hungry.

"The medicine man decides when the corn can be eaten," Wild Jumper say. "To celebrate, we have the Green Corn Dance. That's when we all give thanks to the Great Spirit for all he's given us."

Saturday, July 5, 1834

Memories of the Green Corn Dance will always stay with me. The festival lasted four days, and was like Thanksgiving and Christmas, all in one. Clarissa laughed and played, and took part in 'most everything.

We thanked the Great Spirit before we feasted on new corn and meats roasted over the fire. We played ball games, and Wild Jumper and I danced. Life ain't never been this good.

Even Papa had fun—up until he joined the elders in their discussions. All they talked 'bout was how the U.S. government is trying to force us from our homes here onto a reservation in the Oklahoma Territory. Papa say it'd be the only way the Seminoles could keep us slaves. But if we go, our life will never be the same.

Thursday, November 13, 1834

I go to the far end of our settlement as if I was looking for pigments, but I'm really on the lookout for Wild Jumper. I haven't seen him since just after the Green Corn Dance, and I wonder and worry. The last time I saw him, it was when a group of warriors had gathered. They questioned the elders'—and particularly my father's—judgment. "Why should we go off to some territory called Oklahoma when this is really our land?"

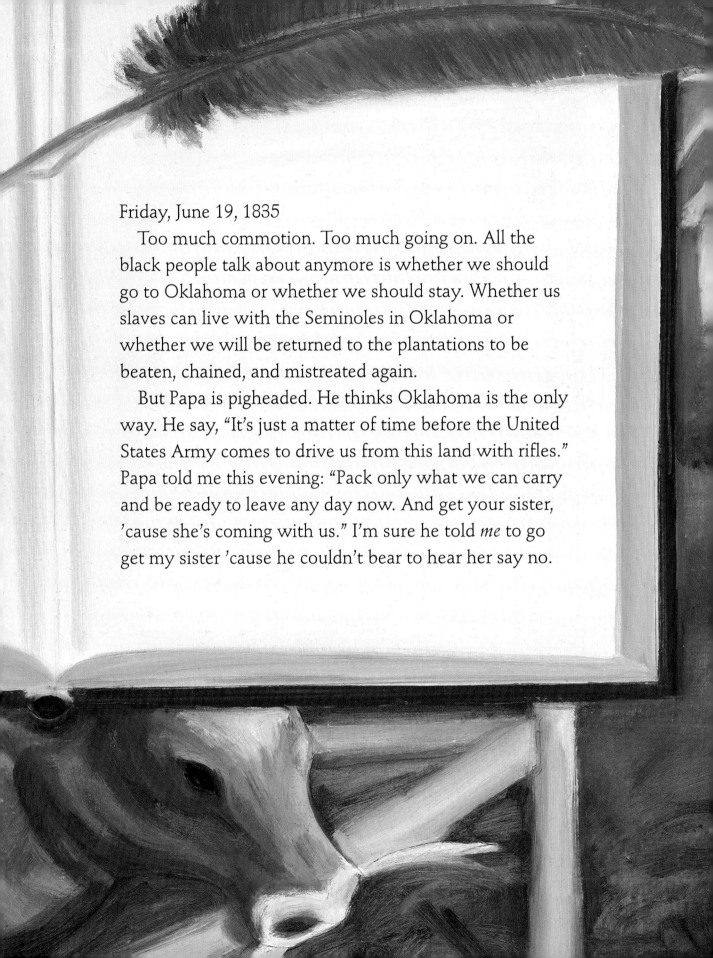

Friday, June 19, 1835

Too much commotion. Too much going on. All the black people talk about anymore is whether we should go to Oklahoma or whether we should stay. Whether us slaves can live with the Seminoles in Oklahoma or whether we will be returned to the plantations to be beaten, chained, and mistreated again.

But Papa is pigheaded. He thinks Oklahoma is the only way. He say, "It's just a matter of time before the United States Army comes to drive us from this land with rifles." Papa told me this evening: "Pack only what we can carry and be ready to leave any day now. And get your sister, 'cause she's coming with us." I'm sure he told *me* to go get my sister 'cause he couldn't bear to hear her say no.

Saturday, June 20, 1835

I go to Honey Flower's home to find Clarissa, but I was told she was sent out to gather sweet grass for baskets. When I turned to search her out, Honey Flower grabbed me by the arm. "Let her go, Libbie. Leave her with me." I was shocked. How could she let her mouth form those words? She was talking about my sister—my family—my blood. "Your father is wrong. Swift Sparrow will never live free in Oklahoma . . . not you . . . not me."

What could I say?

Sunday, June 21, 1835

Me and Papa went to get Clarissa. But Clarissa is gone. Honey Flower is gone. Her husband is gone. And so is half my heart. One old woman told us that most of the settlement has run away to the swamps in South Florida to live on land that even the white man could never want.

I ran crying to search one last time for Wild Jumper, even though I knew in my heart he had left, too. He joined that band of warriors who vowed to fight for the land. How can they possibly fight the U.S. Army and survive? I don't know whose heart is broken more, my papa's or mine.

Monday, June 22, 1835

In just a matter of moments, Papa, Chief Running
Tiger, sixty other Indians and slaves, and I will leave for
the Oklahoma Territory under the armed guard of the
United States Army.

I will probably never see my little sister or Wild
Jumper again. There is nothing more I can say.

Gina's mother closed the book as Gina took a long look at the paintings and other items that lay about their feet. "What happened to those people, Mom? Did everything turn out all right?"

"It's hard to know, Gina. History books tell us that most of the Seminoles and their black slaves were forcibly marched and transported to what was then called Indian Territory in Oklahoma. Their life was not as peaceful as it was in Florida. There were often conflicts with other Indian tribes who were the Seminoles' historic enemies. Often problems arose because other Indians, as well as southern whites, resented the ties of brotherhood shared between the slaves and the Seminoles."

"How about Wild Jumper, Mom? What happened to him?" asked Gina.

"I can't really say for sure. Libbie's diary is all we have. But I do know one of the largest conflicts between United States soldiers and Native Americans occurred during the years eighteen thirty-five to eighteen forty-two, and was known as the Second Seminole War. Many battles were won and lost because a number of Seminole and black warriors chose to stay and fight for their land."

Gina whispered, "And what about Clarissa, Mom? What happened to her?"

"She fled south with Honey Flower's family to the Everglades in southern Florida. A number of their descendants live on some of the Seminole reservations near Miami to this day."

"Miami? Don't we have family in Miami?"

"African Americans have family over much of the world. Wherever there's a desire to live free, wherever there is someone willing to give up his or her life so that we all can be free, we have family."